# GIANT
# TREASURY
## OF
# BEATRIX POTTER

This Book Belongs to:

Charlotte Jane Brennan
from Great Gram Ankli
Oct 1995

# GIANT
# TREASURY
## OF
# BEATRIX POTTER

BY
# BEATRIX POTTER
THE AUTHOR AND ILLUSTRATOR OF *PETER RABBIT*
COMPLETE WITH HER ORIGINAL ILLUSTRATIONS

The Story of a Fierce Bad Rabbit
The Story of Miss Moppet • The Tale of Tom Kitten
The Tale of Jemima Puddle-duck • The Roly-Poly Pudding

Derrydale Books • New York

Originally published as *Beatrix Potter Giant Treasury*.

This edition is published by Derrydale Books,
distributed by Crown Publishers, Inc., 225 Park Avenue South,
New York, New York 10003

Manufactured in the United States of America

Library of Congress Cataloging in Publication Data

Potter, Beatrix, 1866–1943.
   Giant Treasury of Beatrix Potter

   Contents: The story of a fierce bad rabbit—The
story of Miss Moppet—The tale of Tom Kitten—[etc.]
   1. Children's stories, English.   [1. Animals—Fiction]   I. Title.
PZ7.P85Bf   1984      [E]       83-20890
ISBN: 0-517-431211
s   r   q   p   o   n

# CONTENTS

# FOREWORD

Beatrix Potter is one of the best-known writers and illustrators of children's books. Her animal characters are clearly and sharply drawn, endowed with very firm and definite personalities. Her familiarity with the rural life is readily apparent—her animals may wear Edwardian clothes and live in fully furnished homes that any human would be proud to own, but they are still consistent with their natural animal personalities. Jemima Puddle-Duck is easily taken in by a fox with designs on the eggs she is hatching; the kitten Miss Moppet is outwitted by a clever mouse; and Tom Kitten's naturally inquisitive nature lands him in all sorts of predicaments.

Much of Beatrix Potter's appeal lies in her ability to recognize the laws of nature and incorporate them into her stories. She understands that the big fish eats the little fish. Yet her stories are neither cruel nor ruthless. In her classic "Peter Rabbit," Peter and his siblings are warned not to venture into Mr. McGregor's garden because the farmer's wife had cooked Peter's father in a pie. Peter himself barely escapes a similar culinary end. However, the tale is told with wit and humor, and though consistent with the realities of nature, it is neither a sad nor a frightening story.

The five stories collected here, all with their original illustrations, are a charming sample of the work of Beatrix Potter. "The Story of a Fierce Bad Rabbit" shows what happens to a very fierce, very bad rabbit when he behaves poorly toward a gentle rabbit. In "The Story of Miss Moppet" a wily mouse manages to wiggle out of a difficult situation; in "The Tale of Tom Kitten" Tom leads his siblings into antics that crush any hope his mother, Tabitha Twitchit, had of showing off her children at her tea party.

"The Tale of Jemima Puddle-Duck" focuses on a very silly little duck who falls under the spell of a fast-talking fox, eager to "take care" of Jemima's eggs. It requires the canine intelligence of her friend the collie to extricate her, not without some heartache for Jemima. In "The Roly Poly Pudding" Tabatha Twitchit and her family are again featured. Tom Kitten once more causes trouble when he decides to hide from his mother and goes up into the house's huge chimney. Being but a young kitten, he falls victim to a heartless pair of rats who want to wrap him in pie dough and make a meal of him.

Beatrix Potter's stories are loved by both children and adults alike. Children admire the many illustrations, the animals' independence and daring, and sympathize with their inability to do as they are told. Adults appreciate the intricacy and delicacy of Beatrix Potter's drawings and their exquisite detail. They also find that the stories are witty, contain crisp, believable dialogue, and lack any trace of cloying sentimentality. And it is reassuring to adults that while Beatrix Potter is not overtly moralistic, she does make it clear that disobedience usually leads to unpleasant situations.

Anyone familiar with the works of Beatrix Potter will enjoy this *Giant Treasury* and find it a handsome companion to the *Giant Treasury of Peter Rabbit*. For those just discovering the works of this delightful author and artist, the book will serve as a thorough and fascinating introduction.

Anne Ficklen

New York
1983

# THE STORY OF
# A FIERCE
# BAD RABBIT

THIS is a fierce bad Rabbit; look at his savage whiskers and his claws and his turned-up tail.

This is a nice gentle Rabbit. His mother has given him a carrot.

The bad Rabbit would like some carrot.

He doesn't say "Please." He takes it!

And he scratches the good Rabbit very badly.

The good Rabbit creeps away and hides in a hole. It feels sad.

This is a man with a gun.

He sees something sitting on a bench. He thinks it is a very funny bird!

He comes creeping up behind the trees.

And then he shoots—BANG!

This is what happens—

But this is all he finds on the bench
when he rushes up with his gun.

The good Rabbit peeps out of its hole . . .

. . . and it sees the bad Rabbit tearing past—without any tail or whiskers!

THE END

# THE STORY OF
# MISS MOPPET

THIS is a Pussy called Miss Moppet;
she thinks she has heard a mouse!

This is the Mouse peeping out behind the cupboard and making fun of
Miss Moppet. He is not afraid of a
kitten.

This is Miss Moppet jumping just too
late; she misses the Mouse and hits her
own head.

She thinks it is a very hard cup-board!

The Mouse watches Miss Moppet from the top of the cupboard.

Miss Moppet ties up her head in a duster and sits before the fire.

The Mouse thinks she is looking very ill. He comes sliding down the bellpull.

Miss Moppet looks worse and worse. The Mouse comes a little nearer.

Miss Moppet holds her poor head in her paws and looks at him through a hole in the duster. The Mouse comes *very* close.

And then all of a sudden—Miss Moppet jumps upon the Mouse!

And because the Mouse has teased Miss Moppet—Miss Moppet thinks she will tease the Mouse, which is not at all nice of Miss Moppet.

She ties him up in the duster and tosses it about like a ball.

But she forgot about that hole in the duster; and when she untied it—there was no Mouse!

He has wriggled out and run away; and he is dancing a jig on top of the cupboard!

THE END

# THE TALE OF
# TOM KITTEN

DEDICATED

TO ALL

PICKLES,

—ESPECIALLY TO THOSE THAT

GET UPON MY GARDEN WALL

ONCE upon a time there were three little kittens, and their names were Mittens, Tom Kitten, and Moppet.

They had dear little fur coats of their own; and they tumbled about the doorstep and played in the dust.

But one day their mother—Mrs. Tabitha Twitchit—expected friends to tea; so she fetched the kittens indoors, to wash and dress them, before the fine company arrived.

First she scrubbed their faces (this one is Moppet).

Then she brushed their fur (this one is Mittens).

Then she combed their tails and whiskers (this is Tom Kitten).

Tom was very naughty, and he scratched.

Mrs. Tabitha dressed Moppet and Mittens in clean pinafores and tuckers; and then she took all sorts of elegant uncomfortable clothes out of a chest of drawers, in order to dress up her son Thomas.

Tom Kitten was very fat, and he had grown; several buttons burst off. His mother sewed them on again.

When the three kittens were ready, Mrs. Tabitha unwisely turned them out into the garden, to be out of the way while she made hot buttered toast.

"Now keep your frocks clean, children! You must walk on your hind legs. Keep away from the dirty ash-pit, and from Sally Henny Penny, and from the pigsty and the Puddle-ducks."

Moppet and Mittens walked down the garden path unsteadily. Presently they trod upon their pinafores and fell on their noses.

When they stood up there were several green smears!

"Let us climb up the rockery and sit on the garden wall," said Moppet.

They turned their pinafores back to front and went up with a skip and a jump; Moppet's white tucker fell down into the road.

Tom Kitten was quite unable to jump when walking upon his hind legs in trousers. He came up the rockery by degrees, breaking the ferns and shedding buttons right and left.

He was all in pieces when he reached the top of the wall.

Moppet and Mittens tried to pull him together; his hat fell off, and the rest of his buttons burst.

While they were in difficulties, there was a pit pat, paddle pat! and the three Puddle-ducks came along the hard high road, marching one behind the other and doing the goose step—pit pat, paddle pat! pit pat, waddle pat!

They stopped and stood in a row and stared up at the kittens. They had very small eyes and looked surprised.

Then the two duck-birds, Rebeccah and Jemima Puddle-duck, picked up the hat and tucker and put them on.

Mittens laughed so that she fell off the wall. Moppet and Tom descended after her; the pinafores and all the rest of Tom's clothes came off on the way down.

"Come! Mr. Drake Puddle-duck," said Moppet. "Come and help us to dress him! Come and button up Tom!"

Mr. Drake Puddle-duck advanced in a slow sideways manner and picked up the various articles.

But he put them on *himself!* They fitted him even worse than Tom Kitten.

"It's a very fine morning!" said Mr. Drake Puddle-duck.

And he and Jemima and Rebeccah Puddle-duck set off up the road, keeping step—pit pat, paddle pat! pit pat, waddle pat!

Then Tabitha Twitchit came down the garden and found her kittens on the wall with no clothes on.

She pulled them off the wall, smacked them, and took them back to the house.

"My friends will arrive in a minute, and you are not fit to be seen; I am affronted," said Mrs. Tabitha Twitchit.

She sent them upstairs; and I am sorry to say she told her friends that they were in bed with the measles— which was not true.

Quite the contrary; they were not in bed: *not* in the least.

Somehow there were very extraordinary noises overhead, which disturbed the dignity and repose of the tea party.

And I think that some day I shall have to make another, larger book, to tell you more about Tom Kitten!

As for the Puddle-ducks—they went into a pond.

The clothes all came off directly, because there were no buttons.

And Mr. Drake Puddle-duck, and Jemima and Rebeccah, have been looking for them ever since.

THE END

# THE TALE OF
# JEMIMA PUDDLE-DUCK

A FARMYARD TALE

FOR

RALPH AND BETSY

WHAT a funny sight it is to see a brood of ducklings with a hen!

Listen to the story of Jemima Puddle-duck, who was annoyed because the farmer's wife would not let her hatch her own eggs.

Her sister-in-law, Mrs. Rebeccah Puddle-duck, was perfectly willing to leave the hatching to someone else—"I have not the patience to sit on a nest for twenty-eight days; and no more have you, Jemima. You would let them go cold; you know you would!"

"I wish to hatch my own eggs; I will hatch them all by myself," quacked Jemima Puddle-duck.

She tried to hide her eggs; but they were always found and carried off.

Jemima Puddle-duck became quite desperate. She determined to make a nest right away from the farm.

She set off on a fine spring afternoon along the cart road that leads over the hill.

She was wearing a shawl and a poke bonnet.

When she reached the top of the hill, she saw a wood in the distance.

She thought that it looked a safe quiet spot.

Jemima Puddle-duck was not much in the habit of flying. She ran downhill a few yards flapping her shawl, and then she jumped off into the air.

She flew beautifully when she had got a good start.

She skimmed along over the treetops until she saw an open place in the middle of the wood, where the trees and brushwood had been cleared.

Jemima alighted rather heavily and began to waddle about in search of a convenient dry nesting place. She rather fancied a tree stump amongst some tall foxgloves.

But—seated upon the stump, she was startled to find an elegantly dressed gentleman reading a newspaper.

He had black prick ears and sandy colored whiskers.

"Quack?" said Jemima Puddle-duck, with her head and her bonnet on one side—"Quack?"

The gentleman raised his eyes above his newspaper and looked curiously at Jemima—

"Madam, have you lost your way?" said he. He had a long bushy tail which he was sitting upon, as the stump was somewhat damp.

Jemima thought him mighty civil and handsome. She explained that she had not lost her way, but that she was trying to find a convenient dry nesting place.

"Ah! is that so? Indeed!" said the gentleman with sandy whiskers, looking curiously at Jemima. He folded up the newspaper and put it in his coattail pocket.

Jemima complained of the superfluous hen.

"Indeed! How interesting! I wish I could meet with that fowl. I would teach it to mind its own business!

"But as to a nest—there is no difficulty: I have a sackful of feathers in my woodshed. No, my dear madam, you will be in nobody's way. You may sit there as long as you like," said the bushy long-tailed gentleman.

He led the way to a very retired, dismal-looking house amongst the foxgloves.

It was built of faggots and turf, and there were two broken pails, one on top of another, by way of a chimney.

"This is my summer residence; you would not find my earth—my winter house—so convenient," said the hospitable gentleman.

There was a tumbledown shed at the back of the house, made of old soap boxes. The gentleman opened the door and showed Jemima in.

The shed was almost quite full of feathers—it was almost suffocating; but it was comfortable and very soft.

Jemima Puddle-duck was rather surprised to find such a vast quantity of feathers. But it was very comfortable; and she made a nest without any trouble at all.

When she came out, the sandy-whiskered gentleman was sitting on a log reading the newspaper—at least he had it spread out, but he was looking over the top of it.

He was so polite that he seemed almost sorry to let Jemima go home for the night. He promised to take great care of her nest until she came back again next day.

He said he loved eggs and ducklings; he should be proud to see a fine nestful in his woodshed.

Jemima Puddle-duck came every afternoon; she laid nine eggs in the nest. They were greeny white and very large. The foxy gentleman admired them immensely. He used to turn them over and count them when Jemima was not there.

At last Jemima told him that she intended to begin to sit next day—"and I will bring a bag of corn with me, so that I need never leave my nest until the eggs are hatched. They might catch cold," said the conscientious Jemima.

"Madam, I beg you not to trouble yourself with a bag; I will provide oats. But before you commence your tedious sitting, I intend to give you a treat. Let us have a dinner party all to ourselves!

"May I ask you to bring up some herbs from the farm garden to make a savory omelet? Sage and thyme, and mint and two onions, and some parsley. I will provide lard for the stuff—lard for the omelet," said the hospitable gentleman with sandy whiskers.

Jemima Puddle-duck was a simpleton: not even the mention of sage and onions made her suspicious.

She went round the farm garden, nibbling off snippets of all the different sorts of herbs that are used for stuffing roast duck.

And she waddled into the kitchen and got two onions out of a basket.

The collie dog Kep met her coming out, "What are you doing with those onions? Where do you go every afternoon by yourself, Jemima Puddle-duck?"

Jemima was rather in awe of the collie; she told him the whole story.

The collie listened, with his wise head on one side; he grinned when she described the polite gentleman with sandy whiskers.

He asked several questions about the wood and about the exact position of the house and shed.

Then he went out, and trotted down the village. He went to look for two foxhound puppies who were out at walk with the butcher.

Jemima Puddle-duck went up the cart road for the last time, on a sunny afternoon. She was rather burdened with bunches of herbs and two onions in a bag.

She flew over the wood, and alighted opposite the house of the bushy long-tailed gentleman.

He was sitting on a log; he sniffed the air and kept glancing uneasily round the wood. When Jemima alighted he quite jumped.

"Come into the house as soon as you have looked at your eggs. Give me the herbs for the omelet. Be sharp!"

He was rather abrupt. Jemima Puddle-duck had never heard him speak like that.

She felt surprised and uncomfortable.

While she was inside she heard pattering feet round the back of the shed. Someone with a black nose sniffed at the bottom of the door, and then locked it.

Jemima became much alarmed.

A moment afterward there were most awful noises—barking, baying, growls and howls, squealing and groans.

And nothing more was ever seen of that foxy-whiskered gentleman.

Presently Kep opened the door of the shed and let out Jemima Puddle-duck.

Unfortunately the puppies rushed in and gobbled up all the eggs before he could stop them.

He had a bite on his ear, and both the puppies were limping.

Jemima Puddle-duck was escorted home in tears on account of those eggs.

She laid some more in June, and she was permitted to keep them herself: but only four of them hatched.

Jemima Puddle-duck said that it was because of her nerves; but she had always been a bad sitter.

THE END

# THE
# ROLY-POLY PUDDING

IN REMEMBRANCE OF

"SAMMY,"

THE INTELLIGENT PINK-EYED REPRESENTATIVE
OF
A PERSECUTED (BUT IRREPRESSIBLE) RACE.
AN AFFECTIONATE LITTLE FRIEND,
AND MOST ACCOMPLISHED
THIEF!

ONCE upon a time there was an old cat, called Mrs. Tabitha Twitchit, who was an anxious parent. She used to lose her kittens continually, and whenever they were lost they were always in mischief!

On baking day she determined to shut them up in a cupboard.

She caught Moppet and Mittens, but she could not find Tom.

Mrs. Tabitha went up and down all over the house, mewing for Tom Kitten. She looked in the pantry under the staircase, and she searched the best spare bedroom that was all covered up with dust sheets. She went right upstairs and looked into the attics, but she could not find him anywhere.

It was an old, old house, full of cupboards and passages. Some of the walls were four feet thick, and there used to be queer noises inside them, as if there might be a little secret staircase. Certainly there were odd little jagged doorways in the wainscot, and things disappeared at night—especially cheese and bacon.

Mrs. Tabitha became more and more distracted and mewed dreadfully.

While their mother was searching the house, Moppet and Mittens had got into mischief.

The cupboard door was not locked, so they pushed it open and came out.

They went straight to the dough which was set to rise in a pan before the fire.

They patted it with their little soft paws—"Shall we make dear little muffins?" said Mittens to Moppet.

But just at that moment somebody knocked at the front door, and Moppet jumped into the flour barrel in a fright.

Mittens ran away to the dairy and hid in an empty jar on the stone shelf where the milk pans stand.

The visitor was a neighbor, Mrs. Ribby; she had called to borrow some yeast.

Mrs. Tabitha came downstairs mewing dreadfully—"Come in, Cousin Ribby, come in, and sit ye down! I'm in sad trouble, Cousin Ribby," said Tabitha, shedding tears. "I've lost my dear son Thomas; I'm afraid the rats have got him." She wiped her eyes with her apron.

"He's a bad kitten, Cousin Tabitha; he made a cat's cradle of my best bonnet last time I came to tea. Where have you looked for him?"

"All over the house! The rats are too many for me. What a thing it is to have an unruly family!" said Mrs. Tabitha Twitchit.

"I'm not afraid of rats; I will help you to find him; and whip him, too! What is all that soot in the fender?"

"The chimney wants sweeping—Oh, dear me, Cousin Ribby—now Moppet and Mittens are gone!

"They have both got out of the cupboard!"

Ribby and Tabitha set to work to search the house thoroughly again. They poked under the beds with Ribby's umbrella and they rummaged in cupboards. They even fetched a candle and looked inside a clothes chest in one of the attics. They could not find anything, but once they heard a door bang and somebody scuttered downstairs.

"Yes, it is infested with rats," said Tabitha tearfully. "I caught seven young ones out of one hole in the back kitchen, and we had them for dinner last Saturday. And once I saw the old father rat—an enormous old rat— Cousin Ribby. I was just going to jump upon him, when he showed his yellow teeth at me and whisked down the hole.

"The rats get upon my nerves, Cousin Ribby," said Tabitha.

Ribby and Tabitha searched and searched. They both heard a curious roly-poly noise under the attic floor. But there was nothing to be seen.

They returned to the kitchen. "Here's one of your kittens at least," said Ribby, dragging Moppet out of the flour barrel.

They shook the flour off her and set her down on the kitchen floor. She seemed to be in a terrible fright.

"Oh! Mother, Mother," said Moppet, "there's been an old woman rat in the kitchen, and she's stolen some of the dough!"

The two cats ran to look at the dough pan. Sure enough there were marks of little scratching fingers, and a lump of dough was gone!

"Which way did she go, Moppet?"

But Moppet had been too much frightened to peep out of the barrel again.

Ribby and Tabitha took her with them to keep her safely in sight, while they went on with their search.

They went into the dairy.

The first thing they found was Mittens, hiding in an empty jar.

They tipped over the jar, and she scrambled out.

"Oh, Mother, Mother!" said Mittens—

"Oh! Mother, Mother, there has been an old man rat in the dairy—a dreadful 'normous big rat, Mother; and he's stolen a pat of butter and the rolling pin."

Ribby and Tabitha looked at one another.

"A rolling pin and butter! Oh, my poor son Thomas!" exclaimed Tabitha, wringing her paws.

"A rolling pin?" said Ribby. "Did we not hear a roly-poly noise in the attic when we were looking into that chest?"

Ribby and Tabitha rushed upstairs again. Sure enough the roly-poly noise was still going on quite distinctly under the attic floor.

"This is serious, Cousin Tabitha," said Ribby. "We must send for John Joiner at once, with a saw."

Now, this is what had been happening to Tom Kitten, and it shows how very unwise it is to go up a chimney in a very old house, where a person does not know his way, and where there are enormous rats.

Tom Kitten did not want to be shut up in a cupboard. When he saw that his mother was going to bake, he determined to hide.

He looked about for a nice convenient place, and he fixed upon the chimney.

The fire had only just been lighted, and it was not hot; but there was a white choky smoke from the green sticks. Tom Kitten got upon the fender and looked up. It was a big old-fashioned fireplace.

The chimney itself was wide enough inside for a man to stand up and walk about. So there was plenty of room for a little Tom Cat.

He jumped right up into the fireplace, balancing himself upon the iron bar where the kettle hangs.

Tom Kitten took another big jump off the bar and landed on a ledge high up inside the chimney, knocking down some soot into the fender.

Tom Kitten coughed and choked with the smoke; he could hear the sticks beginning to crackle and burn in the fireplace down below. He made up his mind to climb right to the top, and get out on the slates, and try to catch sparrows.

"I cannot go back. If I slipped I might fall in the fire and singe my beautiful tail and my little blue jacket."

The chimney was a very big old-fashioned one. It was built in the days when people burnt logs of wood upon the hearth.

The chimney stack stood up above the roof like a little stone tower, and the daylight shone down from the top, under the slanting slates that kept out the rain.

Tom Kitten was getting very frightened! He climbed up, and up, and up.

Then he waded sideways through inches of soot. He was like a little sweep himself.

It was most confusing in the dark. One flue seemed to lead into another.

There was less smoke, but Tom Kitten felt quite lost.

He scrambled up and up; but before he reached the chimney top he came to a place where somebody had loosened a stone in the wall. There were some mutton bones lying about.

"This seems funny," said Tom Kitten. "Who has been gnawing bones up here in the chimney? I wish I had never come! And what a funny smell? It is something like mouse, only dreadfully strong. It makes me sneeze," said Tom Kitten.

He squeezed through the hole in the wall and dragged himself along a most uncomfortably tight passage where there was scarcely any light.

He groped his way carefully for several yards; he was at the back of the skirting board in the attic, where there is a little mark * in the picture.

All at once he fell head over heels in the dark, down a hole, and landed on a heap of very dirty rags.

When Tom Kitten picked himself up and looked about him, he found himself in a place that he had never seen before, although he had lived all his life in the house.

It was a very small stuffy fusty room, with boards, and rafters, and cobwebs, and lath and plaster.

Opposite to him—as far away as he could sit—was an enormous rat.

"What do you mean by tumbling into my bed all covered with smuts?" said the rat, chattering his teeth.

"Please, sir, the chimney wants sweeping," said poor Tom Kitten.

"Anna Maria! Anna Maria!" squeaked the rat. There was a pattering noise and an old woman rat poked her head round a rafter.

All in a minute she rushed upon Tom Kitten, and before he knew what was happening . . .

. . . his coat was pulled off, and he was rolled up in a bundle, and tied with string in very hard knots.

Anna Maria did the tying. The old rat watched her and took snuff. When she had finished, they both sat staring at him with their mouths open.

"Anna Maria," said the old man rat (whose name was Samuel Whiskers), "Anna Maria, make me a kitten dumpling roly-poly pudding for my dinner."

"It requires dough and a pat of butter and a rolling pin," said Anna Maria, considering Tom Kitten with her head on one side.

"No," said Samuel Whiskers, "make it properly, Anna Maria, with breadcrumbs."

"Nonsense! Butter and dough," replied Anna Maria.

The two rats consulted together for a few minutes and then went away.

Samuel Whiskers got through a hole in the wainscot and went boldly down the front staircase to the dairy to get the butter. He did not meet anybody.

He made a second journey for the rolling pin. He pushed it in front of him with his paws, like a brewer's man trundling a barrel.

He could hear Ribby and Tabitha talking, but they were too busy lighting the candle to look into the chest.

They did not see him.

Anna Maria went down by way of the skirting board and a window shutter to the kitchen to steal the dough.

She borrowed a small saucer and scooped up the dough with her paws.
She did not observe Moppet.

While Tom Kitten was left alone under the floor of the attic, he wriggled about and tried to mew for help.

But his mouth was full of soot and cobwebs, and he was tied up in such very tight knots, he could not make anybody hear him.

Except a spider who came out of a crack in the ceiling and examined the knots critically, from a safe distance.

It was a judge of knots because it had a habit of tying up unfortunate bluebottles. It did not offer to assist him.

Tom Kitten wriggled and squirmed until he was quite exhausted.

Presently the rats came back and set to work to make him into a dumpling. First they smeared him with butter, and then they rolled him in the dough.

"Will not the string be very indigestible, Anna Maria?" inquired Samuel Whiskers.

Anna Maria said she thought that it was of no consequence; but she wished that Tom Kitten would hold his head still, as it disarranged the pastry. She laid hold of his ears.

Tom Kitten bit and spit, and mewed and wriggled; and the rolling pin went roly-poly, roly; roly-poly, roly. The rats each held an end.

"His tail is sticking out! You did not fetch enough dough, Anna Maria."

"I fetched as much as I could carry," replied Anna Maria.

"I do not think"—said Samuel Whiskers, pausing to take a look at Tom Kitten—"I do *not* think it will be a good pudding. It smells sooty."

Anna Maria was about to argue the point when all at once there began to be other sounds up above—the rasping noise of a saw, and the noise of a little dog, scratching and yelping!

The rats dropped the rolling pin and listened attentively.

"We are discovered and interrupted, Anna Maria; let us collect our property—and other people's—and depart at once.

"I fear that we shall be obliged to leave this pudding.

"But I am persuaded that the knots would have proved indigestible, whatever you may urge to the contrary."

"Come away at once and help me to tie up some mutton bones in a counterpane," said Anna Maria. "I have got half a smoked ham hidden in the chimney."

So it happened that by the time John Joiner had got the plank up—there was nobody under the floor except the rolling pin and Tom Kitten in a very dirty dumpling!

But there was a strong smell of rats; and John Joiner spent the rest of the morning sniffing and whining, and wagging his tail, and going round and round with his head in the hole like a gimlet.

Then he nailed the plank down again and put his tools in his bag, and came downstairs.

The cat family had quite recovered. They invited him to stay to dinner.

The dumpling had been peeled off Tom Kitten and made separately into a bag pudding, with currants in it to hide the smuts.

They had been obliged to put Tom Kitten into a hot bath to get the butter off.

John Joiner smelt the pudding; but he regretted that he had not time to stay to dinner, because he had just finished making a wheelbarrow for Miss Potter, and she had ordered two hen coops.

And when I was going to the post late in the afternoon—I looked up the lane from the corner, and I saw Mr. Samuel Whiskers and his wife on the run, with big bundles on a little wheelbarrow, which looked very like mine.

They were just turning in at the gate to the barn of Farmer Potatoes.

Samuel Whiskers was puffing and out of breath. Anna Maria was still arguing in shrill tones.

She seemed to know her way, and she seemed to have a quantity of luggage.

I am sure *I* never gave her leave to borrow my wheelbarrow!

They went into the barn and hauled their parcels with a bit of string to the top of the haymow.

After that, there were no more rats for a long time at Tabitha Twitchit's.

As for Farmer Potatoes, he has been driven nearly distracted. There are rats, and rats, and rats in his barn! They eat up the chicken food, and steal the oats and bran, and make holes in the meal bags.

And they are all descended from Mr. and Mrs. Samuel Whiskers—children and grandchildren and great-great-grandchildren.

There is no end to them!

Moppet and Mittens have grown up into very good rat-catchers.

They go out rat-catching in the village, and they find plenty of employment. They charge so much a dozen and earn their living very comfortably.

They hang up the rats' tails in a row on the barn door, to show how many they have caught—dozens and dozens of them.

But Tom Kitten has always been afraid of a rat; he never durst face anything that is bigger than—

A Mouse.

THE END